About the Author

MICHAEL P. SPRADLIN is the author of several children's picture books, the novels and manga volumes in the Spy Goddess series, and the Youngest Templar novels. He lives in Michigan with his family.

About the Illustrator

JEFF WEIGEL is an author, illustrator, and graphic designer who lives in Belleville, Illinois. He has been a frequent contributor to Image Comics' Big Bang anthology, and is the author and illustrator of the children's picture books *Atomic Ace (He's Just My Dad)*, *Atomic Ace and the Robot Rampage*, and the forthcoming graphic novel *Thunder from the Sea*.

It's Beginning to Look a Lot Like
ZOMBIES!
A Book of Zombie Christmas Carols

Michael P. Spradlin
Illustrations by Jeff Weigel

HARPER

NEW YORK • LONDON • TORONTO • SYDNEY

To my family, Kelly, Mick, and Rachel,
who are definitely not Zombies . . .

HARPER

HarperCollins books may be purchased for educational, business, or sales promotional use. For information please write: Special Markets Department, HarperCollins Publishers, 10 East 53rd Street, New York, NY 10022.

FIRST EDITION

Designed by Justin Dodd
Illustrations by Jeff Weigel

Library of Congress Cataloging-in-Publication Data is available upon request.

ISBN 978-0-06-195643-0

09 10 11 12 13   OV/RRD   10 9 8 7 6 5 4 3 2

CONTENTS

INTRODUCTION

*"Good King Wenceslas tastes great,
we might as well eat Stephen."*

It is universally acknowledged that there are very few literary pursuits which cannot be improved by the addition of Zombies, which are to the written word as cheesy goldfish crackers are to life in general; those little cheesy goldfish crackers also improve nearly everything. Don't take my word for it—just bust out a bowl of cheesy goldfish crackers at the next funeral you attend and see if you don't bring some smiles to the grieving. (Just to be safe, make it the funeral of some stranger on the off chance I'm wrong.)

Imagine how much more compelling *Hamlet* might have been had his father not appeared on the battlements as a ghost but as a brain-eating Zombie. Likewise, how poignant the love story if sweet, damp Ophelia had returned from her drowning in the brook to lay a licking to Hamlet's medulla oblongata. Think how much easier a time wives today would have getting their husbands to take them to the opera if Wagner had only included a few Zombies in his work. Or even a Zombie or two in an Andrew Lloyd Webber musical. (Wait. I'm not sure even Zombies would improve an Andrew Lloyd Webber musical). Even Charles Dickens seems to be overworked with ghosts and short of Zombies. Poor, rotting Tiny Tim having a nosh on Scrooge's brain at the end of *A Christmas Carol* would surely warm the spirit as much as any Christmas goose. I mean, he had four ghosts in the story— couldn't he have substituted at least one Zombie for a ghost? Come on, Chuck. 'Splain, please. Why is there no Zombie of Christmas Future?

And while we're on the subject of Christmas and ghosts and other undead things, I firmly believe it was only a matter of time until someone conceived a book of Zombie Christmas carols. And Michael Spradlin is the ideal guy to do it.

And I can tell you why.

A few years ago, it was the same Michael Spradlin, author of the book you now hold in your hands, who approached *me* one day to write a funny Christmas book. (He was totally violating the restraining order, but we'll let that slide for now.) He got up in my grille and was all, "You know, you ought to write a funny Christmas book." And I'm all, "What kind of funny Christmas book?" And he's all, "I don't know, how about maybe *Christmas in Pine Cove* or something?" (For the uninitiated, Pine Cove is the fictional California town where many of my novels are set.) So I'm all back at him, "'kay." So

I sat down to write my own version of the cheery holiday tale (mainly because I really don't like to write when I'm standing up). But I wanted my holiday novel to be different. I didn't want your traditional Christmas story of happiness and peace on earth and goodwill toward men. (Not that there's anything wrong with that.) But I pondered: How could I make my mine stand out? Then I remembered! What is it that makes every literary pursuit better? Zombies, of course! (See above.) Thus was born my novel *The Stupidest Angel: A Heartwarming Tale of Christmas Terror* (available wherever books are sold, I'm just sayin'). Really, I'm not lying. All because Michael Spradlin got in my grille about shaking up the world of Christmas literature, *The Stupidest Angel*, the cheesy goldfish cracker of holiday novels, was born.

I was to later learn that this same Michael Spradlin, who is himself descended from a long line of the undead (think about it), had a deeper affinity for Zombies than I had even imagined. And now he has brought forth the world's first Zombie Christmas carol songbook. Like collections of greatest hits you see on late-night television commercials, all the new soon-to-be classic Zombie holiday songs are here for you: "I Saw Mommy Chewing Santa Claus"; "Zombie, the Snowman"; "We Three Spleens"; "Deck the Halls with Parts of Wally"; and many more.

So as you and your family enjoy these holiday-spiced tidbits of animated carrion, imagine that you are not gathered around the table waiting for the credit-card bills to descend like the war hammer of a vengeful Santa. Instead, you are all together, barricaded inside your house, stockpiling your supply of canned goods and preparing to fend off hordes of rotting carolers outside. And if one of you should be bitten, well, the more the merrier . . .

"Bring a hatchet for little Nell.
Or a nice pump shotgun will do her well."

Happy Holidays!
Christopher Moore

I'LL BE UNDEAD THIS CHRISTMAS

It's not a question of if.

It's a question of when.

The swine flu. SARS. The Spanish Influenza of 1918—all walks in the park compared to what awaits us. I'm talking of course about the Zombie virus. Right now, scientists are working on the undead around the clock in secret government laboratories to come up with a vaccine for the dreaded bug. Personally, I don't like their chances. And I should also mention that many of these secret government laboratories are located right in your own communities. (After all, Zombie scientists still need to send their children to good schools.) This is only going to cause the virus to spread faster when it breaks.

And it will break.

Their efforts are futile. There is no escaping the Zombie virus. So when the world falls down around us, when we're forced to spend every waking (and sleeping) moment with machetes duct-taped to our hands, let us not forget our most sacred holiday traditions. Just remember that, in the Zombie age, our holidays will be different. Canned goods will become like currency, so don't look for any cranberry sauce on your Christmas table. In the post-Zombie apocalypse, a can of cranberry sauce will bring you at least two shotgun shells from the survivors in the compound across the river.

And you can forget about the traditional lighting of the Yule Log. Use it instead to smash a Zombie's head in. There won't be any time for ceremonies when there are Zombies scratching at your door. You won't be hanging stockings, you'll be wearing them for warmth. Yes, even those tacky ones you get at the mall with your name embroidered on them.

But one tradition that doesn't need to change is the Christmas carol. It only needs to be altered slightly. And that's why you've picked up this book—just to hedge your bets. Because when you are turned (and you will be turned), you won't want to be shunned by all the other Zombies as they gather around a steaming pile of brains. You'll want to know the words to all the Zombie Christmas carols so you can sing along with your new peeps. So pick up a copy. (Or better yet, two or three, since you'll want everyone in your future Zombie family to be prepared.)

Good luck. Happy Holidays. And here's hoping you won't get bitten. Even though you probably will. And here's one last bit of advice: When the virus breaks out and everything around you is going south, just look at the Christmas fruitcake in a new light. No one ever eats them and now you won't need to re-gift them anymore.

You can take a Zombie's head off with one of those suckers.

It's Beginning to Look a Lot Like
ZOMBIES!

I Saw Mommy Chewing Santa Claus

Sung to the tune of "I Saw Mommy Kissing Santa Claus"

I saw Mommy chewing Santa Claus
Underneath the Christmas tree last night.
I snuck up without a peep
Behind Mommy, the Zombie creep,
Now she's biting off Santa Claus's cheek.

When I saw Mommy chewing Santa Claus
Underneath his beard now turning red,
Oh what a laugh we would have said
If Daddy weren't already dead
While Mommy chewed on Santa Claus last night.

Zombies on the Housetop

Sung to the tune of "Up on the Housetop"

Up on the housetop, Zombies pause,
Eating poor old Santa Claus.
Down through the chimney come Santa's parts.
Once a Zombie bites—ouch that smarts!

Chorus
Ho, Ho, Ho, better not go.
Ho, Ho, Ho, better not go.
Up on the housetop, snack, snack, snack.
Down through the chimney comes Santa's back.

First comes the corpse of little Nell.
Oh, those Zombies bit it well.
Forget about a dolly that laughs and cries,
Zombies die first then open their eyes.

Chorus

Next the undead are stalking little Will.
Oh, just see he's a glorious meal.
We use a hammer and lots of tacks,
And he has a brain and a spine that cracks.

Ho, ho ho! Who wouldn't go?
Ho, ho, ho! Who wouldn't go?
Up on the housetop, snack, snack, snack!
Down through the chimney with Santa's back!

We Three Spleens

Sung to the tune of "We Three Kings"

We three spleens, you know where we are:
Two in the kitchen and one in the car.
We are still eating, people are fleeing.
Let's eat the one in the car.

O-oooh, spleens of wonder, they taste right.
We could eat spleens all day and night.
We're still eating, people screaming.
Let's eat until first light.

The Zombie Christmas Song

Sing to the tune of "The Christmas Song (Chestnuts Roasting on an Open Fire)"

Fresh brains roasting on an open fire,
Zombies chewing off your nose—
It all began when they ate the whole choir.
They're even eating Eskimos.

Everybody knows a leg bone and someone's toes
Make a Zombie's season bright.
Tiny tots, with their eyes in a bowl,
Will find it hard to see tonight!

We know Zombie Santa's on his way;
He's eaten lots of boys and girls in his sleigh,
And every mother's child is going to spy
To see if Zombie reindeer really know how to fly.

And so I'm running to get out of here
Before the Zombies eat me too.
Although it's been said about the Undead,
If you don't run, they will feast on you.

Undead Christmas

Sung to the tune of "Blue Christmas"

I'll have an undead Christmas without you.
I'll be so undead, and not thinking about you.
Hanging lots of red brains on a green Christmas tree
Won't mean a thing if you're not undead with me.

I'll have an undead Christmas, that's certain.
And when that Zombie bites me, I'm hurtin'.
You'll be running all night, from every Zombie in sight,
And I'll have an undead, undead Christmas.

It's Beginning to Look a Lot Like Zombies

Sung to the tune of "It's Beginning to Look a Lot Like Christmas"

It's beginning to look a lot like Zombies
Everywhere you go.
They're in the five and ten, eating brains once again,
Faces smeared with blood and all aglow!
It's beginning to look a lot like Zombies!
They're in every store!
But the scariest sight to see is the Zombies that will be
At your own front door.

There's no need for boots, or a pistol that shoots,
Just the brains of Barney and Ben.
Zombies will stalk when you go for your walk,
And they'll eat Janice and Jen.
And Mom and Dad, already turned, are eating brains again.

It's beginning to look a lot like Zombies
Everywhere you go.
They've stormed the Grand Hotel, and filled the park as well.
They're hungry and they sure don't mind the snow!
It's beginning to look a lot like Zombies!
Blood splattered on the floor!
But the scariest sight to see is the Zombies that will be
At your own front door!

Nothing Like Brains for the Holidays

Sung to the tune of "There's No Place Like Home for the Holidays"

Oh there's nothing like brains for the holidays!
No matter how far away you roam,
When you're hungry for the taste
Of someone else's face,
For the holidays, you can't beat
Brains, sweet brains!

I ate a man who lived in Tennessee,
And he was headed for Pennsylvania,
To go eat his mother's eye.
From Pennsylvania folks are traveling down
To Dixie's sunny shore.
From Atlantic to Pacific, gee!
The cerebrum tastes terrific!

Oh there's nothing like brains
For the holidays! 'Cause no matter
How much your own mouth foams,
If you want to be happy in a million ways,
For the holidays, you can't beat
Brains, sweet brains.

Zombie Wonderland

Sung to the tune of "Winter Wonderland"

Undead moan, are you listening?
In the lane, blood is glistening.
A horrible sight,
We're screaming tonight,
Runnin' through a Zombie wonderland.

Already turned, is our neighbor!
Zombies here, I belabor.
They moan their own song,
As we scream along,
Sprintin' through a Zombie wonderland.

In the meadow, we can beg for mercy.
They've already eaten Parson Brown.
They'll come for us next,
And we'll say, "No man!"
We're getting' the hell
Out of this town.

Later on, we'll perspire,
As we scream, by the fire.
I'll say we're afraid
Of the Zombies they've made,
Runnin' through a Zombie wonderland.

Good King Wenceslas Tastes Great

Sung to the tune of "Good King Wenceslas"

Good King Wenceslas tastes great;
We might as well eat Stephen,
When the brains lay round about,
Toasted crisp and bleedin'.
Brightly shown the moon that night,
Though the virus cruel.
When a poor man came in sight,
He made fine undead fuel.

Hither, Zombies chase after her.
Agnes, she is yelling.
Yonder peasant, how she screams,
For her brains they're a-jelling.
Surely she will try to hide
Underneath the mountain,
Or deep in the forest hence
While Agnes is digestin'.

Bring me flesh, and bring me brains.
Bring me Zombies hither.
Thou and I will see them dine;

They even bite through leather.
Free and screaming, forth they went,
Zombies right behind them,
Through the poor souls' wild lament.
Bitter brains are better.

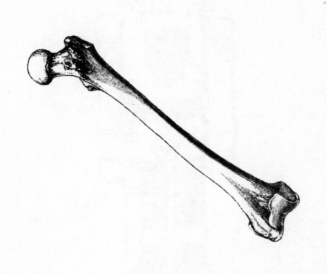

Have Yourself a Medulla Oblongata

Sung to the tune of "Have Yourself a Merry Little Christmas"

Have yourself a medulla oblongata!
Let's eat something light.
Have you tried,
The hippocampus? It's out of sight!

Have yourself a medulla oblongata!
Make the Yuletide gray,
From now on,
We'll just eat frontal lobes all day.

Here we are as in undead days,
Happy golden days of gore.
Flesh and brains are what's dear to us,
So let's eat some up, once more.

Through the screams,
We all will eat together,
If the brains allow,
Hang a hypothalamus upon the highest bough,
And have yourself a medulla oblongata now.

Here Comes Zombie Claus

Sung to the tune of "Here Comes Santa Claus"

Here comes Zombie Claus, here comes Zombie Claus,
Right down Zombie Claus Lane!
Vixen and Blitzen and his undead reindeer
are eating all the brains.
Bells are ringing, children screaming;
All is bloody and bright.
Load your shotgun and say your prayers,
'Cause Zombie Claus comes tonight.

Here comes Zombie Claus, here comes Zombie Claus,
Right down Zombie Claus Lane!
He's got a bag that is filled with brains,
And we don't know where he's been.
Hear those sleigh bells jingle-jangle.
What a horrible night.
Jump in bed, hold onto your head,
'Cause Zombie Claus comes tonight.

Here comes Zombie Claus, here comes Zombie Claus,
Right down Zombie Claus lane.
He doesn't care if you're rich or poor;
He'll eat you just the same.
Zombie Claus knows we're all just protein;

That makes everything right.
So fill your shotgun up with shells
'Cause Zombie Claus comes tonight!

Here comes Zombie Claus, here comes Zombie Claus,
Right down Zombie Claus Lane!
He'll come around when the screams ring out
That there're fresh brains again.
Zombie virus will come to all
If we just cower in fright.
So let's give thanks to Smith and Wesson,
'Cause Zombie Claus comes tonight!

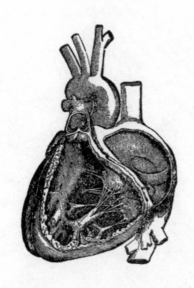

Snacking Around the Christmas Tree

Sung to the tune of "Rockin' Around the Christmas Tree"

Snacking around the Christmas tree
at the undead party hop.
Missing toes hung where you can see,
chewy eyeballs just go pop!

Chorus
Noshing around the Christmas tree,
Don't let the humans get away.
Later we'll have some fresh skull pie
And some undead caroling.

You will get a sentimental feeling, for your ear
It's gone now but you're still jolly,
The halls are decked with parts of Wally.

Chorus

Snacking around the Christmas tree,
Have a munchy holiday.
Zombies dancing merrily,
In the new old-fashioned way.

SLAY RIDE

Sung to the tune of "Sleigh Ride"

Chorus I

Just hear those fresh brains jingling,
And nostrils running with goo.
Come on, it's lovely weather
To go flesh-eating together with you.

Chorus II

Outside the bodies are falling
And Zombies are calling "woo-hoo."
Come on, it's lovely weather
To go flesh-eating together with you.

Take a bite, take a bite, take a bite, let's go.
Here's a leg with a shoe,
We're riding in a wonderland of ooze.

Take a chomp, take a chomp, take a chomp, it's grand;
An ear's in my hand.
We're gliding along with a song
Of a Zombie wonderland.

Their cheeks are nice and tasty,
And brains are basting you see.
We're snuggled up together
Like two flesh-eaters would be.

Let's take that road before us
And eat a chorus or two.
Come on, it's lovely weather
To go flesh-eating together with you.

There's a Zombie party at the home of Farmer Gray.
His brain'll be the perfect ending of a perfect day;
We'll be eating the parts we love to eat without a single stop
At the fireplace while we watch the eyeballs pop.
Pop! Pop! Pop!

There's a happy feeling nothing in the world can buy
When they pass around a femur and somebody's eye—
It'll be just like a picture print by undead Currier and Ives.
These wonderful brains are the brains
We'll be eating all through our lives!

Chorus I & II

It's lovely weather to go flesh-eating together with you.
It's lovely weather to go flesh-eating together with you.

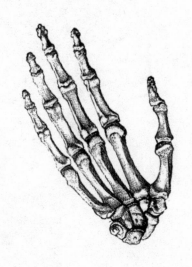

A Jolly Zombie Christmas

Sung to the tune of "A Holly, Jolly Christmas"

Have a jolly Zombie Christmas;
Time to eat somebody's ear.
I don't know if we'll eat toes,
But they'll still scream in fear.
Have a jolly Zombie Christmas,
And when they run down the street,
Say hello to friends you know
And bite ev'ryone you meet.

Oh, ho,
There's poor Joe, hung where you can see.
Somebody waits for you;
Bite her once for me.
Have a Jolly Zombie Christmas,
And in case you lose your ears,
Oh, by golly,
Have a jolly
Zombie Christmas this year.

Deck the Halls with Parts of Wally

Sung to the tune of "Deck the Halls with Boughs of Holly"

Deck the halls with parts of Wally,
Fa la la la la, la la la la.
'Tis the season for brains by golly,
Fa la la la la, la la la la.

Chew we now our friend's gray matter,
Fa la la, fa la la, la la la.
Wear old clothes 'cause fresh brains splatter,
Fa la la la la, la la la la.

See the blazing town before us,
Fa la la la la, la la la la.
Let's go in and eat the chorus,
Fa la la la la, la la la la.

Follow me, we eat with leisure,
Fa la la, fa la la, la la la.
A fresh brain for our Yuletide pleasure.
Fa la la la la, la la la la.

Zombie, the Snowman

Sung to the tune of "Frosty, the Snowman"

Zombie the Snowman was a jolly, happy ghoul,
With a corncob pipe and some boy's nose
And two eyes he got at school.

Zombie the Snowman is a fairy tale, they say;
He was undead, it's so,
But the children know how he came back to life one day.

There must have been a virus in
That old silk hat they found,
For when they placed it on his head,
He began to dance around.

Oh, Zombie the Snowman was alive as he could be,
And the children say he ate brains all day,
And they ran from that Zombie.

Chorus
Thumpety thump thump,
Thumpety thump thump,
Look at Zombie go.
Thumpety thump thump,
Thumpety thump thump,
Over the hills of snow.

Zombie the Snowman knew the brains were fresh that day,

So he said, "Please run, because it's lots more fun when I eat
your brain that way."

Down through the village with a femur in his hand,

Running here and there all around the square,

Sayin', "Decapitate me if you can!"

He chased them through the streets of town

And ate the traffic cop,

And he barely paused a moment when he heard the cop's brain
pop!

Zombie the Snowman

Had to hurry on his way,

But he waved good-bye, sayin', "Please do cry,

I'll eat your brains someday!"

Chorus

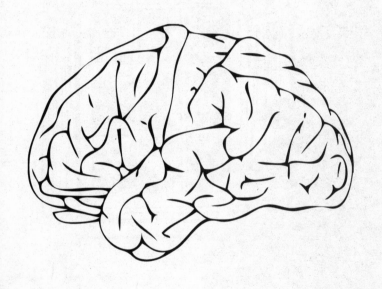

Eat a Toe

Sung to the tune of "Let It Snow"

Oh the virus outside is spreadin',
And there's more and more undeadin',
But when fresh brains are running low,
Eat a toe! Eat a toe! Eat a toe!

The Zombie 'pocalypse ain't stopping—
Listen, hear the eyeballs a-popping,
But fresh brains are running low,
Eat a toe! Eat a toe! Eat a toe!

The humans put up a good fight,
But lost out to a Zombie swarm!
So if you'll really let me turn,
I'll eat my own sister's arm!

Civilization is slowly dying,
And, humans, we're still good-bying,
But Zombies already ate your nose,
Eat a toe! Eat a toe! Eat a toe!

Here We Come A-Garroting

Sung to the tune of "Here We Come A-Caroling"

Here we come a-garroting,
Among the brains that bleed.
Here we come a-Zombie-ing,
Undead to be seen.

Chorus
We have come to eat you,
With a Zombie virus, too.
And God bless you as I rip off your ear,
And God bless you as I rip off your ear.

We are not your normal Zombies
Who roam from door to door,
But we were friendly neighbors,
Whom you have seen before.

Chorus

Let's eat the master of this house,
And eat the mistress too,
And all the little children,
Let's eat them through and through.

Chorus

And all your kin and kinfolk
That dwell both far and near,
We wish they were still living,
But they are gone we fear.

Chorus

I'm Dreaming of an Undead Christmas

Sung to the tune of "I'm Dreaming of a White Christmas"

I'm dreaming of an undead Christmas,
With the virus all aglow,
Where the brainpans glisten
And humans listen
To hear Zombies tromping through the snow.

I'm dreaming of an undead Christmas
With every human that I bite.
May your days be merry and bright,
And may all your Christmas brains taste right.

I'm dreaming of an undead Christmas
With every human being I bite.
May your days be scary with fright,
And may all your Christmas brains taste right.

Zombie Yells

Sung to the tune of "Jingle Bells"

Bleeding from the nose,
There's one horse left to slay,
O'er the fields we go,
Feasting all the way.
Bells on bobtails ring,
Make undead spirits bright.
What fun it is to chew and sing
An eating song tonight!

Oh, Zombie yells, Zombie yells,
Howling all the way.
Oh, what fun it is to ride
In an undead open sleigh!
Zombie yells, Zombie yells,
Chomping all the way.
Oh, what fun it is to ride
In an undead open sleigh!

A day or two ago,
I got a Zombie bite,
And soon Miss Fanny Bright—
I was chewing on her side.
The horse was lean and stank,

But horse brains are our lot.
We got into a drifted bank
And the horse he was upsot.

Oh, Zombie yells, Zombie yells,
Howling all the way!
Oh, what fun it is to ride
In an undead horsey sleigh!
Zombie yells, Zombie yells,
Chomping all the way.
Oh, what fun it is to ride
In an undead horsey sleigh, yeah!

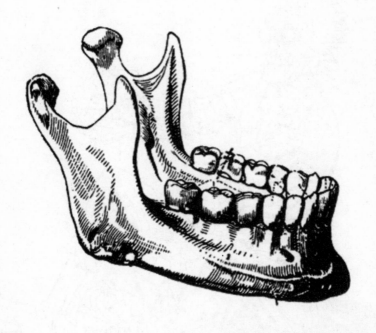

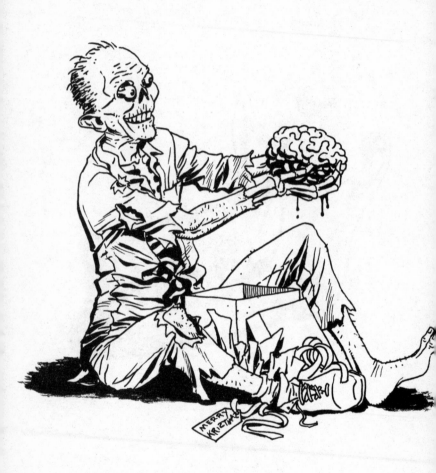

Let's Feast on Merry Gentlemen

Sung to the tune of "God Rest Ye Merry Gentlemen"

Let's feast on merry gentlemen;
There'll be arterial spray.
Remember, eat your vegetables
With brains on Christmas Day.
You can't be saved from Zombie's power;
Undead have gone astray.
Eating brains brings us comfort and joy,
Comfort and joy,
O, eating brains brings us comfort and joy.

SILVER BRAINS

Sung to the tune of "Silver Bells"

City sidewalks, busy sidewalks,
Simply teeming with brains!
In the air
There's a new
Zombie virus.
Undead laughing,
Brains they're passing,
Eating mile after mile,
And on ev'ry street corner you'll hear:

Silver brains! Silver brains!
It's undead party time in the city.
Do our thing! Hear them scream!
The Zombie will carry the day!

All the streetlights,
Even stoplights,
No longer blink red and green
As the shoppers become barricaders!

Hear the bones crunch,
See the kids munch,
Even on Santa we feed.
And above all the gristle
You'll hear:

Let's eat brains, silver brains!
It's undead party time in the city.
Do our thing, hear them scream!
Soon it will be Christmas Day.

I'll Be Undead for Christmas

Sung to the tune of "I'll Be Home For Christmas"

I'll be undead for Christmas,
Eating more than I usually do,
And although I know it's a long road home,
I'll be fueled by goo.

Chorus
Christmas Eve will find me
Wherever brains will be.
I'll be undead for Christmas,
When I hear your screams.

I'll be undead this Christmas—
Yes the virus, it got me.
Tramp through the snow, to eat some toes
And brains under the tree.

Chorus

When I hear your screams.
When I hear your screams.

Grandma Got Turned into a Zombie

Sung to the tune of "Grandma Got Run Over by a Reindeer"

Chorus
Grandma got turned into a Zombie,
Walking home from our house Christmas Eve.
You can say there's no such thing as Undead.
But as for me and Grandpa, we believe.

She'd been drinkin' too much eggnog,
And we'd begged her not to go.
But she ignored our Zombie warnings,
And she staggered out the door into the snow.

When we found her Christmas mornin'
At the scene of the attack,
She was missing part of her forehead,
And incriminatin' undead marks were on her back.

Chorus

Now we're all so proud of Grandpa.
He's been takin' this so well;
See him in there with a sharp machete,
Drinkin' beer and loadin' his shotgun up with shells.

It's not Christmas without Grandma;
All the family waits for her attack,
And we just can't help but wonder:
Should we decapitate her with a whack?

Chorus

Now Grandma's out there clawing at the window,
And Grandpa, he doesn't give a fig.
He will take his sharp machete,
And chop right down through Grandma's blue-haired wig.

I've warned all my friends and neighbors,
Better stock up your pantry shelves.
The Undead surely are a menace,
And some of them look like their former selves.

Chorus

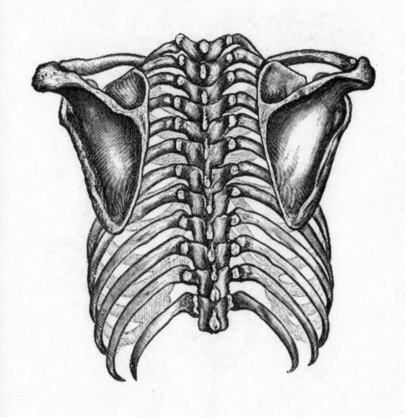

It's the Most Wonderful Time to Feel Fear

Sung to the tune of "It's the Most Wonderful Time of the Year"

It's the most wonderful time to feel fear,
While the virus is jelling,
And everyone's yelling that Zombies are here,
It's the most wonderful time to feel fear.

There'll be fresh brains for roasting,
Intestines for toasting,
And body parts out in the snow.
There'll be Undead beheading
And Zombies a-spreading,
From viruses long, long ago.

It's the most wonderful time to feel fear.
There'll be no Zombies slowing,
And brains will be glowing,
When undead ones are near.
It's the most wonderful time to feel fear!

We Wish You an Undead Christmas

Sung to the tune of "We Wish You a Merry Christmas"

Chorus

We wish you an undead Christmas;

We wish you an undead Christmas;

We wish you an undead Christmas while we chew off your ear.

Zombie virus we bring to you and your kin;

We'll eat brains for Christmas and through the New Year.

Oh, bring us a hippocampus;

Oh, bring us a hippocampus;

Oh, bring us a hippocampus and a cup of root beer.

We won't go until we eat you;

We won't go until we eat you;

We won't go until we eat you, so come on out here.

Chorus

Smash Their Heads with a Rock

Sung to the tune of "Jingle Bell Rock"

Zombies yell, Undead smell, heads smashed with rocks,
Human guts swing, and hear them all scream,
Snarling and growling as the humans all run—
Now the Zombie hop has begun.

Zombies yell, undead smell, heads smashed with rocks,
Jingle bells chime in Zombie hell time.
Dancing and prancing, Zombies beware;
They're in the frosty air.

What a virus! It's inside us.
They'll eat our brains all day.
Virus time is a swell time
To get the hell out of here any old way.
Giddy-up jingle horse, pick up your feet,
Zombies are on our block.

Mix and a-mingle with their shuffling feet.
Here the Zombies yell,
We're in undead hell.
Smash their heads with a rock!

Rudolph, the Zombie Reindeer

Sung to the tune of "Rudolph, the Red-Nosed Reindeer"

He ate Dasher, then Dancer,
Then Prancer and Vixen.
He downed Comet and Cupid
And Donner and Blitzen.
Yes, he ate them all, the most
Famous undead reindeer of all:

Rudolph, the Zombie reindeer,
Caught the virus through his nose.
And if you ever saw him,
You would even say he's gross.

All of the other reindeer
Tried real hard to get away.
But they didn't count on Rudolph
Eating them anyway.

Then one foggy Christmas Eve,
Santa came to say:
"Rudolph, with your Zombie blight,
Who's gonna pull my sleigh tonight?"

Rudolph instead just ate him,
Munching Santa's brain with glee,
Rudolph, the Zombie reindeer,
You changed Christmas history!

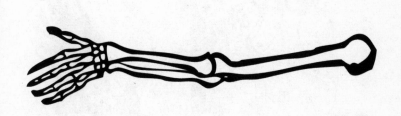

All I Want for Christmas Is to Be a Zombie

Sung to the tune of "All I Want for Christmas Is My Two Front Teeth"

Every body pauses and stares at me,
I'm a pile of rotting flesh as you can see.
It looks like a virus caused this catastrophe!
But my one wish on Christmas Eve is to be a Zombie!

All I'll eat for Christmas
Is your frontal lobe,
Your frontal lobe,
With my two front teeth!

Gee, if I could only
Eat your frontal lobe,
Then more Zombies would spread around the globe.

It seems so long since I've been undead;
Sister Susie's a rotting hag!
Gosh oh gee, how happy I'd be,
If only there were more brains to be had!

All I want for Christmas
Is to be a Zombie,
To be a Zombie,
To be a Zombie.

Gee, if I could only
Be a Christmas Zombie,
Then I could eat you
On Christmas Day!

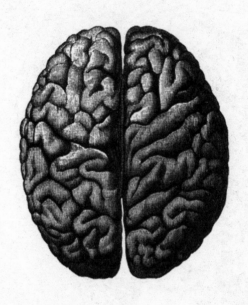

Zombie Claus Is Coming to Town

Sung to the tune of "Santa Claus Is Coming to Town"

You better watch out,
You better not cry,
Better not shout,
Or he'll know where you hide—
Zombie Claus is coming to town!

He's eating a wrist
And chewing it twice;
A little fresh brain with pepper is nice.
Zombie Claus is coming to town!

He eats you when you're sleeping;
He bites when you're awake.
He chews if you've been bad or good,
So just hide for goodness' sake!

O, you better watch out,
You better not cry,
Better not shout,
Or he'll know where you hide.
Zombie Claus is coming to town!
Zombie Claus is coming to town!